A Place for Sam

Written by

Shawn Elizabeth George

Illustrated by

Jan Z. Cohen

This book is dedicated to...

Kate, Gavin, Matthew

& my nieces and nephews,

May you grow to know your place and purpose.

May you live fully as the person you were made to be.

Love,

Mom/Aunt Shawn

My children, nieces, nephews and students...

Enjoy the journey as you find your place in this world.

With love,

J.Z.C

Sam is puzzled.

She doesn't know
where she belongs.

She doesn't quite fit in here...

...or
over
there.

But she wants to.

So she's keeps trying to *SQUEEZE* herself into this space or that place.

She simply doesn't fit.

Sam's heart is
sad.

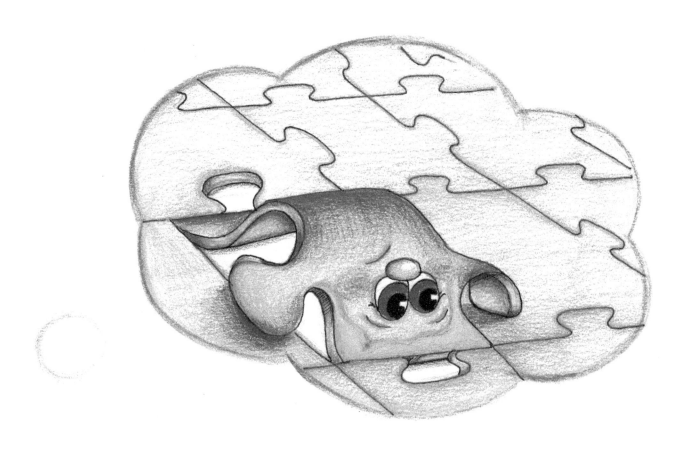

She wants to change who she is.

She wants to change how she was made.

Christopher, the puzzle maker, saw Sam
wandering around. His heart was sad
for Sam. He had made Sam exactly
as she was and knew she had a
place and a purpose in his puzzle.

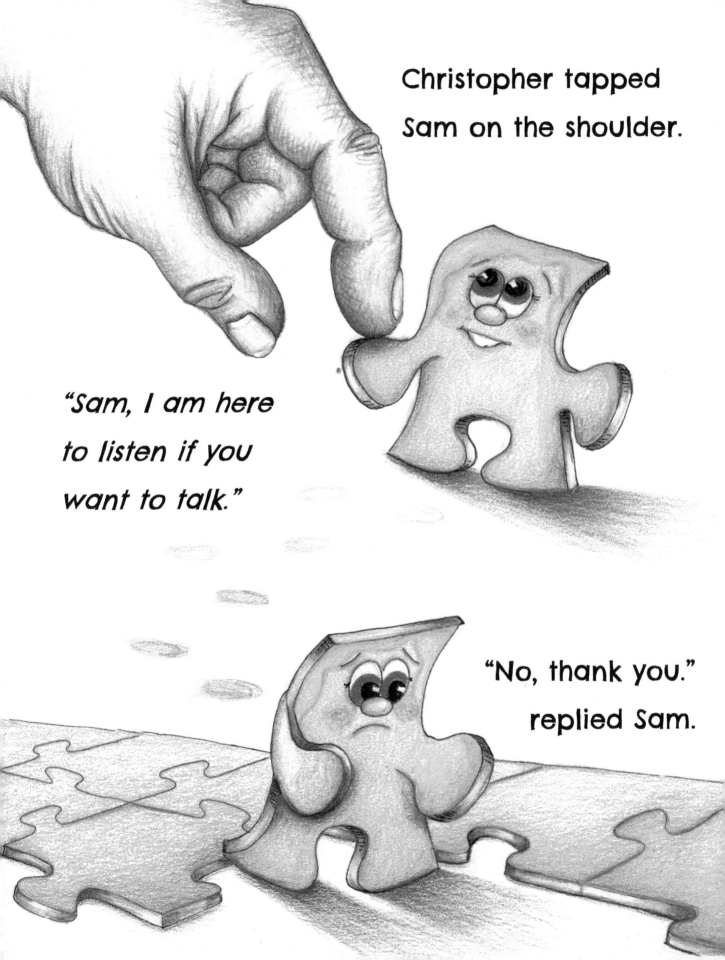

Christopher tapped Sam on the shoulder.

"Sam, I am here to listen if you want to talk."

"No, thank you." replied Sam.

Christopher stepped back and watched
Sam continue to wander...

...searching for her place in the puzzle.

Sam looked at the other pieces fitting in and she wondered why she couldn't be like them.

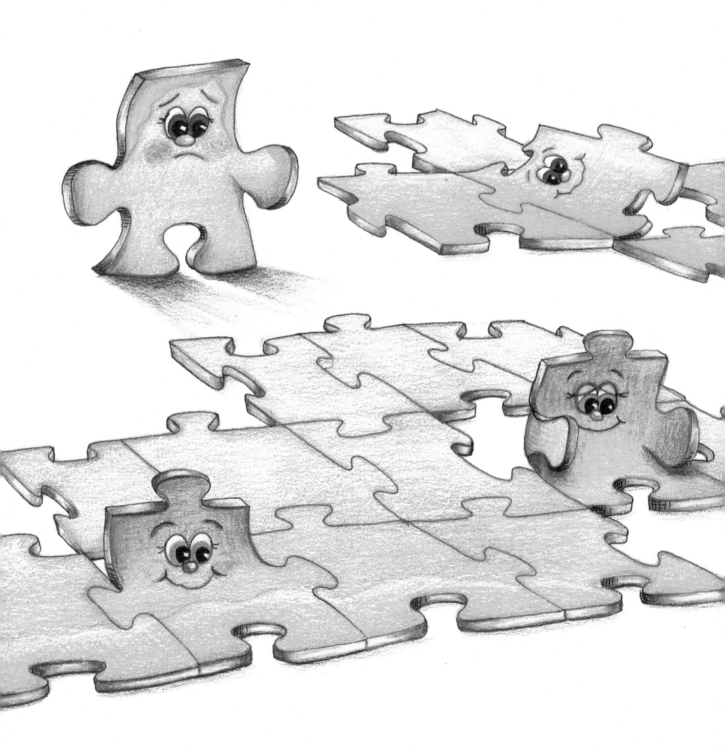

Disheartened, Sam fell down
and called out to Christopher,

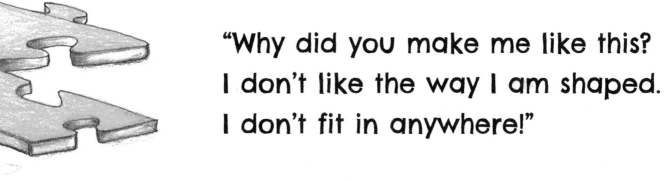

"Why did you make me like this?
I don't like the way I am shaped.
I don't fit in anywhere!"

To her surprise, Christopher was right there listening.

"Sam, I hear you."

"Then please do something to change me," cried Sam.

"I made you the way you are
with a place and a purpose.

Trust me.

Stop trying to change who
you are and start looking to
become who you are,"
responded Christopher.

Sam looked up.

Bewildered she asked,

"I have a place and a purpose?"

"Yes, you do."

"How do I find it?"
Sam questioned.

"Keep talking with me and I will guide you there," Christopher said with love.

Sam was tired of wandering aimlessly and figured she would give it a try.

She continued walking and talking with Christopher.

They walked....

...and talked.

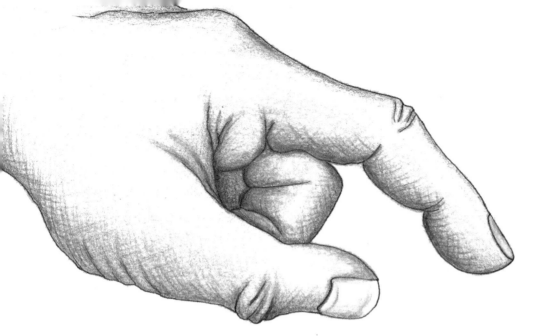

And he held true to his promise,

guiding Sam along the way.

One day Sam was lost in conversation when
to her surprise Christopher said calmly,

"You're home."

Sam paused and looked around.
She saw that there was an empty place
in the puzzle where he had guided her.

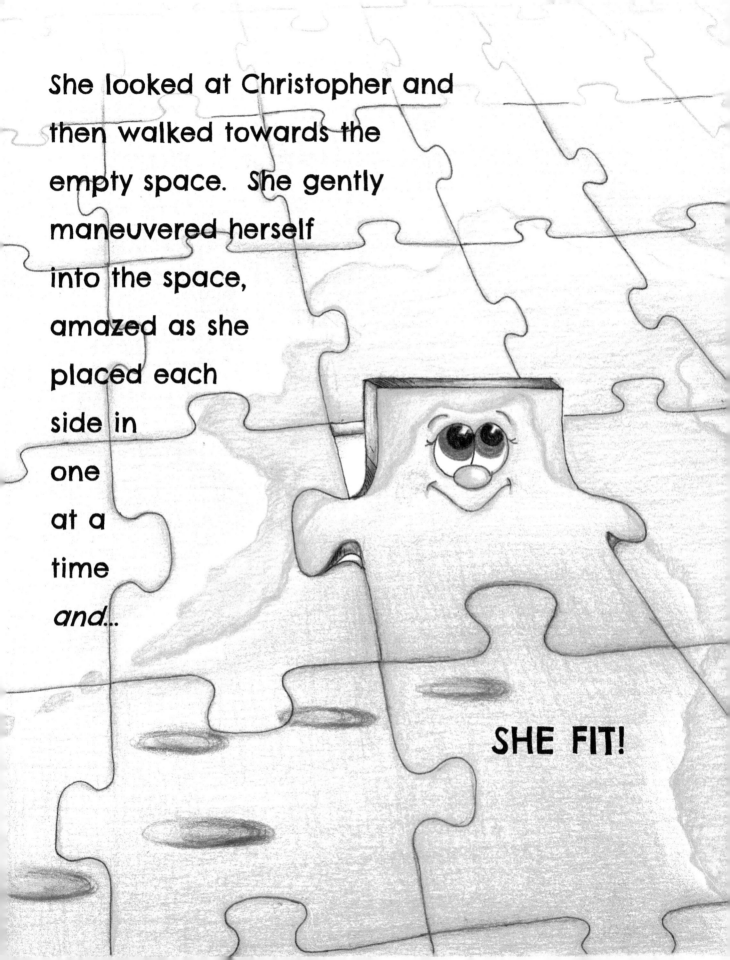

She looked at Christopher and then walked towards the empty space. She gently maneuvered herself into the space, amazed as she placed each side in one at a time *and...*

SHE FIT!

SAM FIT!

Sam found her place!

She found her home!

She didn't need to be different
than how she was made!

Sam realized the puzzle
wouldn't be complete without her;
just as she was shaped, just as she was made.

Sam has a place!
Sam has a purpose!

Her place was right here
and her purpose was to
connect with the other puzzle
pieces so the whole puzzle
would be complete.

With a joyful heart Sam said,

"Thank you, Christopher."

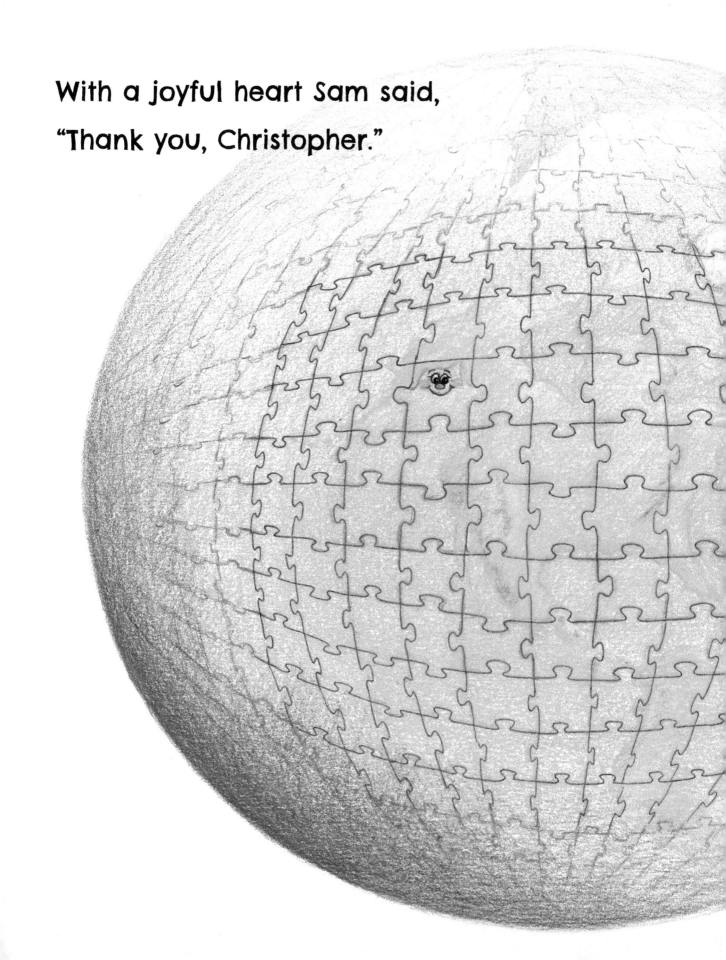

Christopher smiled at
his beautiful creation,
grateful that Sam had found
her place and purpose in his puzzle.

Sam's piece of the puzzle matters.

And yours does too!

You are wonderfully made,

inside and out.

Questions from Sam...

- What was your favorite part of my story? Why?

- Who was your favorite character in the story? Why?

- What were some of the problems I had during the story?

- How did I change throughout the story?

- Who is Christopher?

- What are three words you would use to describe Christopher?

- Name some of the emotions I had during the story.

- Do you ever feel some of those emotions too?

- Choose two emotions you share with me and when you feel them.

- Did my problem get solved? How?

- What do you think the main message of my story is?

- What was the most interesting thing you learned from my story?

- Why do you think the author wrote this book for you?

- What is something you learned from me that you can apply in your life?

Visit Sam at www.aplaceforsam.com

CPSIA information can be obtained
at www.ICGtesting.com
Printed in the USA
BVOW10s0500041216
469733BV00026B/712/P